KU-365-854

Material in this book was previously published in Ladybird's
Nursery Rhymes gift book.

Ladybird books are widely available, but in case of
difficulty may be ordered by post or telephone from:

Ladybird Books – Cash Sales Department
Littlegate Road Paignton Devon TQ3 3BE
Telephone 01803 554761

A catalogue record for this book is available
from the British Library

Published by Ladybird Books Ltd Loughborough Leicestershire UK
Ladybird Books Inc Auburn Maine 04210 USA

PLAYTIME
RHYMES

Chosen by Ronne Randall
Illustrated by Peter Stevenson

Girls and boys, come out to play,
The moon is shining bright as day.
Leave your supper and leave your sleep,
And come with your playfellows
  into the street.
Come with a whoop, and come with a call,
Come with a good will, or come not at all.
Come, let us dance on the open green,
And she who holds longest shall be our queen.

One for the money,
Two for the show,
Three to make ready,
And four to go!

I love sixpence, jolly, jolly sixpence,
    I love sixpence as my life.
I spent a penny of it, I spent a penny of it,
    I took a penny home to my wife.

I love fourpence, jolly, jolly fourpence,
    I love fourpence as my life.
I spent twopence of it, I spent twopence of it,
    I took twopence home to my wife.

I love nothing, jolly, jolly nothing,
    I love nothing as my life.
I spent nothing of it, I spent nothing of it,
    I took nothing home to my wife.

Up and down the City Road,
In and out the Eagle,
That's the way the money goes,
Pop goes the weasel!

Half a pound of tuppenny rice,
Half a pound of treacle,
Mix it up and make it nice,
Pop goes the weasel!

Follow my Bangalorey Man,
Follow my Bangalorey Man,
I'll do all that ever I can
To follow my Bangalorey Man.

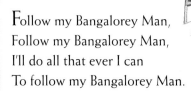

Oh, do you know the muffin man,
    The muffin man, the muffin man?
Oh, do you know the muffin man
    That lives in Drury Lane?

I'm a little teapot,
Short and stout,
Here is my handle,
Here is my spout.
When I see the teacups,
Hear me shout,
"Tip me over and
   pour me out!"

Polly put the kettle on,
Polly put the kettle on,
Polly put the kettle on,
   We'll all have tea.

Sukey take it off again,
Sukey take it off again,
Sukey take it off again,
   They've all gone away.

One, two, three,
I love coffee,
And Billy loves tea.
How good you be,
One, two, three,
I love coffee,
And Billy loves tea.

There were three cooks of Colebrook,
And they fell out with our cook.
And all was for the pudding he took
From the three cooks of Colebrook.

Oranges and lemons,
Say the bells of St Clement's.
You owe me five farthings,
Say the bells of St Martin's.
When will you pay me?
Say the bells of Old Bailey.
When I grow rich,
Say the bells at Shoreditch.
Pray, when will that be?
Say the bells of Stepney.
I'm sure I don't know,
Says the great bell at Bow.

Here comes a candle to light you to bed,
And here comes a chopper to chop off your head!

London Bridge is falling down,
Falling down, falling down.
London Bridge is falling down,
My fair lady.

Build it up with iron bars,
   etc.

Iron bars will bend and break,
   etc.

Build it up with gold and silver,
   etc.

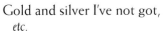

Gold and silver I've not got,
   etc.

Then off to prison you must go,
You must go, you must go.
Then off to prison you must go,
My fair lady.

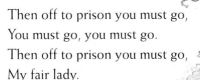

Humpty Dumpty sat on a wall,
Humpty Dumpty had a great fall.
All the King's horses
And all the King's men
Couldn't put Humpty together again.

Ride a cockhorse to Banbury Cross,
To see a fine lady upon a white horse.
Rings on her fingers,
And bells on her toes,
And she shall have music
    wherever she goes.

Jack be nimble,
Jack be quick.
Jack jump over
The candlestick.

Here am I,
Little jumping Joan.
When nobody's with me,
I'm all alone.

Leg over leg,
As the dog went to Dover.
When he came to a stile,
Hop! He went over.

13

This is the way the ladies ride,
Nimble, nimble, nimble, nimble.
This is the way the gentlemen ride,
A gallop, a trot, a gallop, a trot.
This is the way the farmers ride,
Jiggety-jog, jiggety-jog.

Up at Piccadilly, oh!
The coachman takes his stand,
And when he meets a pretty girl,
He takes her by the hand.
Whip away for ever, oh!
Drive away so clever, oh!
All the way to Bristol, oh!
He drives her four-in-hand.

"Robert Barnes, my fellow fine,
Can you shoe this horse of mine?"
"Yes, indeed, that I can,
As well as any other man.
There's a nail, and there's a prod,
And now, you see, your horse
     is shod!"

Cobbler, cobbler, mend my shoe,
Get it done by half-past two.
Do it neat, and do it strong,
And I will pay you when it's done.

One, two,
Buckle my shoe,

Three, four,
Knock at the door.

Five, six,
Pick up sticks,

Seven, eight,
Lay them straight.

Nine, ten,
A big fat hen,

Eleven, twelve,
Dig and delve.

Thirteen, fourteen,
Maids a-courting,

Fifteen, sixteen,
Maids in the kitchen.

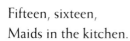

Seventeen, eighteen,
Maids in waiting,

Nineteen, twenty,
My plate's empty.

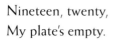

Ride, baby, ride,
Pretty baby shall ride,
And have a little puppy dog tied to his side,
And a little pussy cat tied to the other,
And away he shall ride to see his grandmother.

You ride behind and I'll ride before,
And trot, trot away to Baltimore.
You shall take bread, and I will take honey,
And both of us carry a purse full of money.

Hogs in the garden, catch 'em, Towser.
Cows in the cornfield, run, boys, run.
Cats in the cream pot, run, girls, run.
Fire on the mountains,
  run, boys, run!

See-saw, Margery Daw,
Jacky shall have a new master.
Jacky shall have but a penny a day,
Because he can't work
  any faster.

See-saw, sacra down,
Which is the way to Boston town?
One foot up, the other foot down,
That is the way to Boston town.

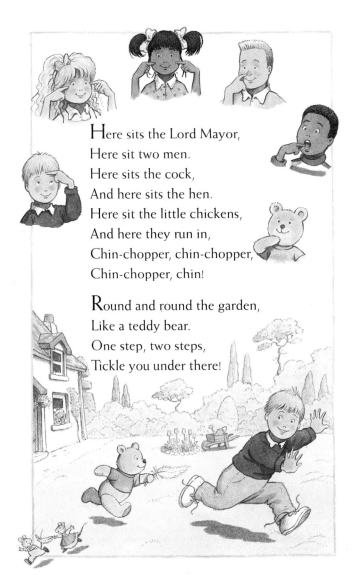

Here sits the Lord Mayor,
Here sit two men.
Here sits the cock,
And here sits the hen.
Here sit the little chickens,
And here they run in,
Chin-chopper, chin-chopper,
Chin-chopper, chin!

Round and round the garden,
Like a teddy bear.
One step, two steps,
Tickle you under there!

How many days has my baby
  to play?
Saturday, Sunday, Monday,
Tuesday, Wednesday,
Thursday, Friday,
Saturday, Sunday, Monday.
Hop away, skip away,
My baby wants to play,
My baby wants to play every day!

Dance to your daddy,
My little babby,
Dance to your daddy,
My little lamb!
You shall have a fishy
In a little dishy,
You shall have a fishy
When the boat comes in!

One, two, three, four, five,
Once I caught a fish alive.
Why did you let it go?
Because it bit my finger so.

Six, seven, eight, nine, ten,
Shall we go to fish again?
Not today, some other time,
For I have broke my fishing line.

Three wise men of Gotham
Went to sea in a bowl.
If the bowl had been stronger,
My song would be longer!

The big ship sails on the alley, alley O,
The alley, alley O, the alley, alley O.
The big ship sails on the alley, alley O,
On the last day of September.

The big ship sank to the bottom of the sea,
The bottom of the sea, the bottom of the sea.
The big ship sank to the bottom of the sea,
On the last day of September.

We all dip our heads in the deep blue sea,
The deep blue sea, the deep blue sea.
We all dip our heads in the deep blue sea,
On the last day of September.

One, two, three, four,
Mary at the kitchen door.
Five, six, seven, eight,
Eating cherries off a plate.

One's none,
Two's some,
Three's many,
Four's a penny,
Five's a little hundred.

Three little ghostesses,
Sitting on postesses,
Eating buttered toastesses,
Greasing up their fistesses,
Up to their wristesses.

Little Tommy Tucker
Sings for his supper.
What shall he eat?
White bread and butter.

How will he cut it
Without e'er a knife?
How will he marry
Without e'er a wife?

Little Jack Horner
Sat in a corner,
Eating his Christmas pie.
He put in his thumb,
And pulled out a plum,
And said,
    "What a good boy am I!"

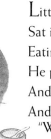

Little Betty Blue
Lost her holiday shoe.
What can little Betty do?
Give her another,
To match the other,
And then she may walk in two.

One leaf for fame, one leaf for wealth,
One for a faithful lover,
And one leaf to bring glorious health,
Are all in a four-leaf clover.

One, he loves; two, he loves;
Three, he loves, they say.
Four, he loves with all his heart;
Five, he casts away.
Six, he loves; seven, she loves;
Eight, they both love.
Nine, he comes; ten, he tarries;
Eleven, he courts; twelve, he marries.

To market, to market, to buy a fat pig,
Home again, home again, jiggety-jig.
To market, to market, to buy a fat hog,
Home again, home again, jiggety-jog.

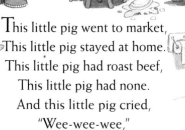

This little pig went to market,
This little pig stayed at home.
This little pig had roast beef,
This little pig had none.
And this little pig cried,
"Wee-wee-wee,"
All the way home.